This 1997 edition is published by Derrydale Books,
a division of Random House Value Publishing, Inc.,
40 Engelhard Avenue, Avenel, New Jersey 07001.

Random House
New York • Toronto • London • Sydney • Auckland
http://www.randomhouse.com/

Printed in Italy

TRAVEL BACK IN TIME

story by
Vezio Melegari

illustrations by
Giovanni Giannini
Violayne Hulné

DERRYDALE BOOKS
NEW YORK • AVENEL, NEW JERSEY

VIRTUAL REALITY

Believe me: Benny Felicity is one smart puppy. With
his friends and other young students, Walt Wolfsbane
has formed a "virtual reality" club.
Today they're visiting the laboratory of Walt's father,
Professor Alfred E. Wolfsbane.
"Virtual reality," explains the professor, "is something
that is there but isn't really there, something that no
longer exists but that can be seen, something that once
was and that, thanks to us, can be again!"
Did you understand all of that? Not really? Well,
judging from the look of things, it's clear that virtual
reality has something to do with computers, videos,
electronics, and all their magic!

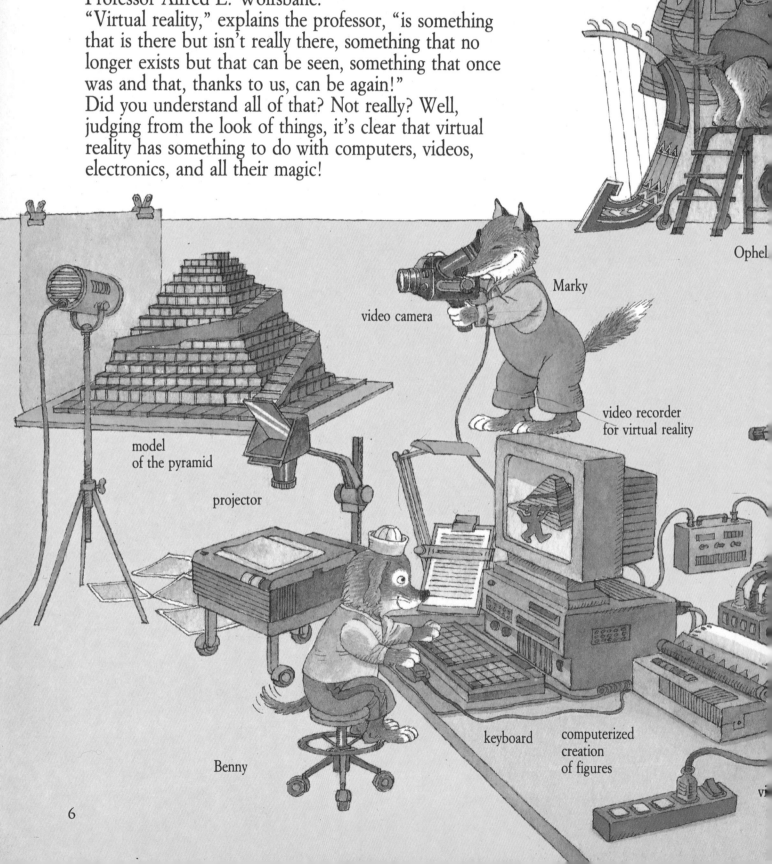

costumes

Ophel

video camera

Marky

video recorder
for virtual reality

model
of the pyramid

projector

Benny

keyboard

computerized
creation
of figures

Hillary

laser projector
for virtual reality

video

Horatio

Walt

Professor
Wolfsbane

Megan

disks

Isidore

7

THE PYRAMIDS OF EGYPT

"Virtual reality is just a trick with images," says Professor Wolfsbane. Then, *click!* he starts the machine, and suddenly men appear, busy at work in the sands of the desert.

"We're in ancient Egypt!" exclaims the kitten Isidore, clapping his paws.

"And those men certainly deserve applause," comments his sister, Hillary. "They're hauling enormous, heavy blocks of stone. They seem to be building something."

architect

slaves

The professor

Isidore

Nile River

8

ding
yramid

scribe

blocks
of stone

pyramid

sphinx

desert

servants

pharaoh

musicians

"Something big and eternal," says the professor. "They're building the famous pyramids, which were tombs for their kings, the pharaohs. Unlike the homes of the time, which were made of wood and bricks, the pyramids were made of stone and are still standing, five thousand years after they were built!"

9

Horatio

STONEHENGE

The virtual reality of Egypt disappears. Where are we now?

"Who are those men in the middle of those enormous stones?" asks the little fox named Marky.

"They're the early ancestors of today's Englishmen," says Hillary. "The stones are the temple of Stonehenge, where they brought gifts to their gods. Stonehenge is almost the same age as the pyramids."

"That's right," says the professor. "Like the ancient

Marky   Isidore   Benn

10

horseshoe-shaped ring
of megaliths

outer ring
of megaliths

moon

Megan

Ophelia

The professor   Hillary

Egyptians, it was very hard for these people to build this temple. It is made up of eighty-two enormous stones called megaliths. They are arranged so that when the light of the sun or the moon strikes they create precise shadows that change according to the hour and minute of the day or night. Stonehenge was a temple for their gods but also a clock!"
"Where do you wind it?" asks Walt. Being the professor's son he tries to get away with jokes, much to his father's annoyance.

columns

Benny

Megan

Marky

Ophelia

Horatio

THE PARTHENON

"The pyramids and Stonehenge," says the professor,
"were already two thousand years old when –"
"– the Parking Song was built!" interrupts Walt.
"The *Parthenon*," corrects his father, giving Walt a
truly wolfish glare. "This is the Par-the-non, and those
girls are honoring the goddess to whom the temple was
dedicated: Athena, the goddess of wisdom. In fact, we

The professor

pediment

procession
of Athenian
girls

Hillary

warrior

Isidore

are now in Athens, in Greece. More precisely, we're on the Acropolis, the highest point of the city, a place full of temples and beautiful buildings!"
"What a wonderful sight!" says Megan.
Then everyone is quiet as they silently enjoy one of the most beautiful corners of the world, created by people during one of the great periods of history.

13

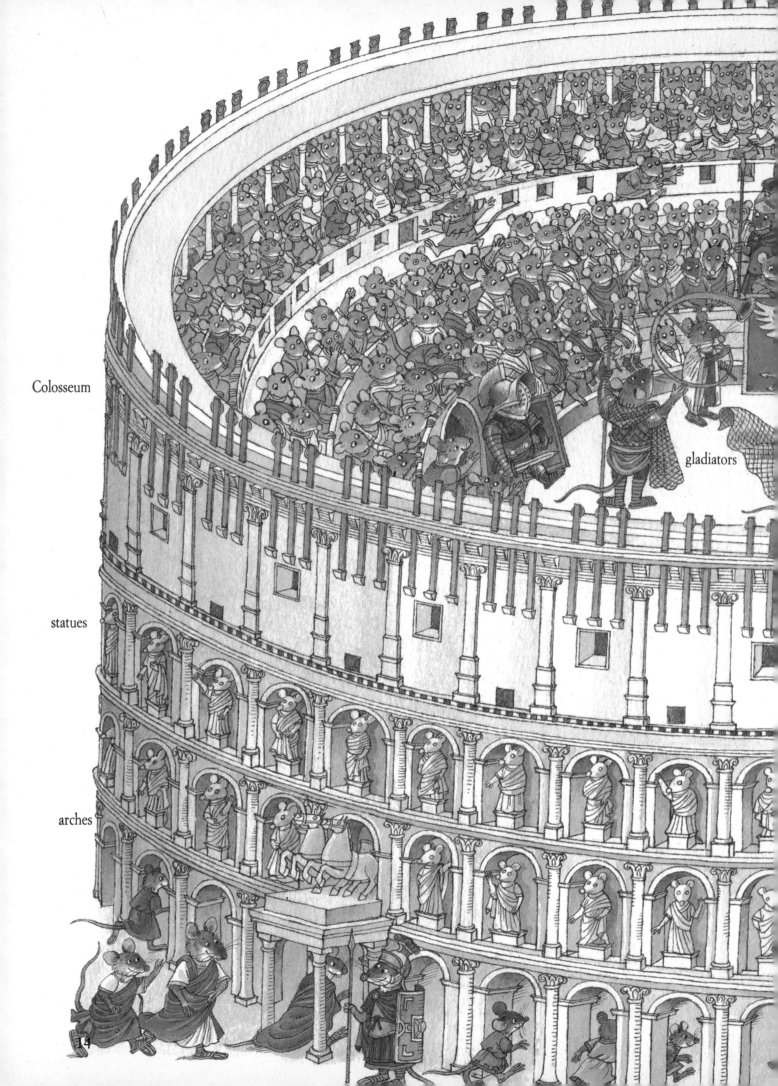

Colosseum

gladiators

statues

arches

14

Hillary

Marky

Megan

The professor

THE COLOSSEUM

toga

"And now we'll go back to two thousand years ago," says the professor. "Let's put on togas and follow the ancient Romans to the biggest theater in their city."

"But this is the Colosseum," says Horatio.

"That's right," says the professor. "And right now warriors called gladiators are engaged in battle. Sometimes they fought with wild animals and –"

"Couldn't we enter some virtual reality just as nice but a little less violent?" break in Horatio and Ophelia, Benny's brother and sister puppies.

"Certainly," says the professor, "but every lesson from history is worth remembering." And with a *click* of his remote control the virtual reality changes.

Ophelia

15

Walt   Horatio

THE GREAT WALL OF CHINA

"Why haven't we seen anything Chinese yet?" asks Hillary. "I've often heard that the Chinese invented everything long before anyone else."

arrow

Ophelia

Marky

Horatio

shield

helmet

sword

guard tower

Isidore

Hillary

Walt

The professor

Benny

spear

road on the Great Wall

Chinese
archer

bow

Mongolian
horseman

loophole

Megan

"That's not completely true," says the professor, "but it is true that if we go back seventeen hundred years we'll find the Chinese building the largest man-made structure in the world: the famous Great Wall of China, made as a defense against the barbarian tribes of the steppe. About six hundred years ago it was reinforced to protect China from the Mongolians. It is also a road and is nearly fifteen hundred miles long."

"I wish I knew how to say 'Great Wall' in Chinese," sighs Benny.

"It's called *Ciang-ceng*," says the professor, "which means 'Long Wall.'"

"*Ciang-ceng! Ciang-ceng*" everyone calls out together.

THE TOWER OF PISA

"Why is everyone running?" asks Walt. "Is a big game about to begin?"

"No, the Tower of Pisa is leaning," answers the professor. "We're back in 1173. In that big field today called Miracle Square – the Pisans were building a bell tower when the ground beneath it gave way."

"It's a good thing the ground stopped giving way and the tower is still standing," says Ma

bells

tower

Hillary

Megan

Ophelia

18   architect   Horatio

cypresses

Pisans

cathedral

baptistery

Miracle
Square

"Unfortunately, that isn't the case," explains the
professor. "The Tower of Pisa keeps leaning more
and more and today is nearly sixteen feet off the
perpendicular."
"Can't anyone straighten it out?" asks Hillary.
"There are no fewer than eleven thousand theories
for how to save it, but for the moment everyone
enjoys photographing it just the way it is!"

Marky   The professor   Walt   19

THE TOWER OF LONDON

"Right in the middle of the capital of Great Britain," announces Professor Wolfsbane, "stands the noble Tower of London. The horseman is William the Conqueror and the men parading after him are his Norman soldiers. It was William, nine hundred years ago, who built the White Tower, still the heart of the fortress."

"Fortress or royal palace?" asks Isidore.

"To tell the truth," says Megan, "it looks more like a prison to me."

"And in fact it was," says the professor. "First for people and then for animals."

"And what are those big black birds flying all around?" asks Benny.

Benny

raven

Hillary

Ophelia

William
the Conqueror

20

"You should be more respectful of the ravens of the Tower of London," cautions the professor. "According to legend, if they left the tower it would fall into ruin, and with it England!"

White Tower

battlement

Viking ship

Thames River

bridge

Norman soldiers

Horatio

Marky

21

Sierra Nevada

tower

colonnade

harquebus

The professor

Isidore

THE ALHAMBRA

"After the fortress with black ravens," says the professor, "let's visit the so-called red fortress, the famous buildings of the Alhambra in Granada, Spain. When Christopher Columbus left on his voyage of discovery in 1492, the kings of Spain had just freed the city of Granada from the rule of the Arabs who had occupied Spain for several centuries."

"What pretty columns!" exclaims Ophelia.

Hillary

Marky

22

halberd

battlement

sentry

fan

sword

Benny

Megan

hat

Horatio

"In fact," continues the professor, "the Alhambra was built by the Arabs, and they decorated it with the ornate designs typical of their art, which are called arabesques."

"Arabesques make me hungry," declares Walt. When Ophelia gives him a questioning glance, he explains, "They remind me of the swirls my mother makes with cream on cakes."

Ophelia   Walt

23

THE FABLED TAJ MAHAL

Professor Wolfsbane pushes a button and continues: "This monumental tomb made of white marble is the Taj Mahal and is in India. It was made about three hundred years ago by an emperor for his beloved wife, who had died at a young age. Its walls are adorned with precious stones. Furthermore, it has four minarets."

"Unless I'm mistaken," interrupts Megan, "minarets are those high towers from which, five times each day,

muezzin

sentry

minaret

architect

Marky

Hillary

Ophelia

Benny

The professor

Megan

Horatio

Isido

dome

the muezzin, the Muslim priest, calls the faithful to prayer."
"One of the minarets is still under construction," says the professor, "and they're building it so that it will lean slightly away from the building instead of standing perfectly straight. Can you guess why? Because that way should it ever happen to fall, it wouldn't hit the Taj Mahal but would fall away from it!"

minaret under construction

palanquin

Walt   elephant

THE PALACE OF VERSAILLES

"Now we're entering a building where there once was a king, and what a king he was! He had himself called the Sun King!" says the professor, pushing another button.

"But this is the royal palace of Versailles!" exclaims Megan.

"Quite right," says the professor. "And a great show is about to begin – the king is going to have lunch! The food is brought to him by waiters and butlers escorted by armed soldiers. The procession leaves the kitchen in the rear of the palace and, after going along paths and crossing courtyards, enters the halls, salons, and vestibules of the palace. As the procession goes by, the courtiers salute it by raising their hats, bowing, and murmuring, "The meat of the king!""

pike

oboe

flute

viola

musicians

Mark

fan

wig

Megan

Horatio

Ophelia

Isidore

Sun King

The professor

Benny

majordomo

waiters

"Well, what is the king having for lunch?" Benny wants to know.

"Four different first courses, then a duck stuffed with truffles, some mutton with garlic, ham, and fruit pies," says the professor.

"Too bad it's only 'virtually' real," exclaims Walt.

27

THE BRANDENBURG GATE

Professor Wolfsbane's virtual reality now reconstructs a colorful and festive military parade from the past. The colors of the uniforms, plumes in the headdresses, and flapping banners bring us back two hundred years. The columns past which the soldiers are parading have just been built. We are in Berlin, historical capital of Germany. The city's most celebrated monument is a gate. Yes, a gate, but different from those that opened, and sometimes still open, in the walls of ancient cities.

drummers

dragoo

banner

chariot

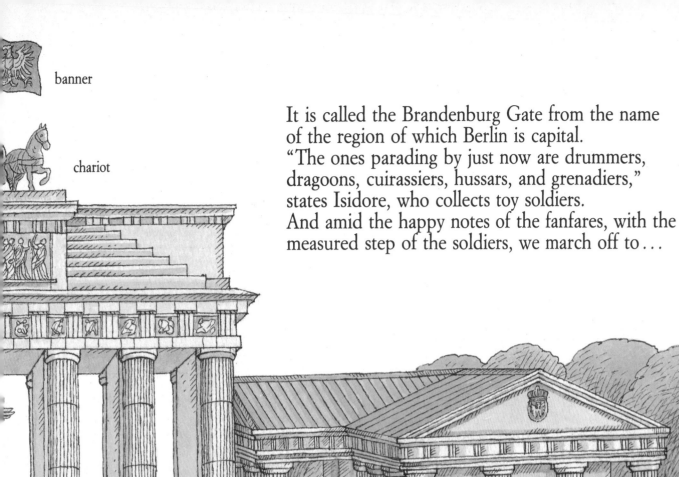

It is called the Brandenburg Gate from the name of the region of which Berlin is capital.
"The ones parading by just now are drummers, dragoons, cuirassiers, hussars, and grenadiers," states Isidore, who collects toy soldiers.
And amid the happy notes of the fanfares, with the measured step of the soldiers, we march off to...

linden trees

cuirassiers

hussars

grenadiers

pavilion
of the Universal
Exposition

fireworks

bridge

Seine
River

30

THE EIFFEL TOWER

"Paris! A name full of magic!" exclaims the professor. "And truly magical is the Eiffel Tower, the city's iron pyramid, and we're invited to its inauguration. But today, March 31, 1889, marks not only the opening of the tower but also of the Universal Exposition, an international fair at which all the world's new technologies will be on display. That's the reason for this iron tower, with its almost three thousand steps."

"As well as four elevators," points out Megan, "that go all the way to the top, where one can see the *Ville Lumière*, the City of Light, as the French proudly call Paris."

hot-air balloon

Right Bank

top hat

wicker gondola

Left Bank

ballast sacks

anchor and line

torch

Empire State
Building

crown

THE STATUE
OF LIBERTY

C.

cruise ship

Hillary

Megan

Benny

Walt

Marky

The pro

32

Twin Towers
of the World
Trade Center

Manhattan

oast
uard

tug boat

THE STATUE OF LIBERTY

"The Statue of Liberty!" yell the friends. And no
wonder. Everyone recognizes the beautiful female
figure at the entry to the port of New York
holding a torch high in the air.
"It's really her," says the professor. "She's been
there since 1886. If you climb all the way to her
crown or the torch you can see the best view
of all the skyscrapers!"
"What is the statue made of?" asks Marky.
"It's made of sheets of copper over an iron
framework. The Statue of Liberty was designed by
the French sculptor Frédéric Bartholdi, and its full
name is *Liberty Enlightening the World*."

flag

binoculars

Isidore

Horatio

Ophelia

skate
board

33

THE SYDNEY OPERA HOUSE

"We've made it to the end of our voyage through virtual reality," announces the professor. "Our last stop will be a theater: the Opera House of Sydney in Australia! But it isn't just an opera house: the building also houses a concert hall, a recording studio, and a movie theater."

"It looks like a sailboat, so white and surrounded by the sea," says Benny.

Pacific
Ocean

"You're right," says the professor. "Its roof is made of ten 'sails,' or domes, of concrete. And it's four times heavier than the Eiffel Tower since the sails are covered by a million ceramic tiles."

domes

"It would take a lot of wind to move a sailboat like that!" exclaims Walt, and all the friends laugh. Even his father, the professor, laughs. He gives his son a loving pat, and then the curtain falls on the virtual reality.

rry
oat

Tower
of London

Parthenon

Alhambra

Taj Mahal

O

Megan

Brandenburg
Gate

Horatio

Palace
of Versailles

Colosseum

Pyram

Walt

Sydney Opera
House

Statue
of Liberty

Stonehenge

Marky

Eiffel
Tower

Hillary

Isidore

Benny

Tower
of Pisa

Great Wall
of China

BEHIND THE CURTAIN

What is behind the curtain? Of course.
The storehouse for the models of all the buildings and
monuments we have seen and visited thanks to
Professor Wolfsbane's electronic tricks! He explains,
"In order to have you visit the places of the past, all I
had to do was film these models and show them as
computer images. Then I animated them with drawings
of the people of the period and pictures of us."
The friends give him a round of applause. "A true
voyage in time," exclaims Benny. And the professor
concludes: "And now, a snack for everyone. After
virtual reality, the Wolfsbane family invites you go
enjoy the very real reality of a monumental chocolate
cake covered with arabesques of cream!"

The professor

cake

CONTENTS

6 VIRTUAL REALITY
8 THE PYRAMIDS OF EGYPT
10 STONEHENGE
12 THE PARTHENON
15 THE COLOSSEUM
16 THE GREAT WALL OF CHINA
18 THE TOWER OF PISA
20 THE TOWER OF LONDON
22 THE ALHAMBRA
24 THE FABLED TAJ MAHAL
26 THE PALACE OF VERSAILLES
28 THE BRANDENBURG GATE
31 THE EIFFEL TOWER
33 THE STATUE OF LIBERTY
34 THE SYDNEY OPERA HOUSE
37 BEHIND THE CURTAIN